I SPY

A BOOK OF
PICTURE
RIDDLES

Photographs by **Walter Wick**
Riddles by **Jean Marzollo**

cartwheel books™

An imprint of Scholastic Inc.
New York

For Linda
W.W.

Book design by Carol Devine Carson

TABLE OF CONTENTS

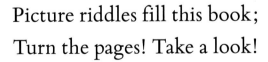

Picture riddles fill this book;
Turn the pages! Take a look!

Use your mind, use your eye;
Read the rhymes and play **I SPY**!

I spy a rabbit, eleven bears in all,
A dog on a block, a seal on a ball;

One red bottle, one rubber band,
A wooden craftstick, and the letters in HAND.

I spy a lion and eight other cats,
A shell from the ocean, a fish who wears hats;

A horse that rocks and a horse that rolls,
A button with a square and one without holes.

I spy a shovel, a long silver chain,
A little toy horse, a track for a train;

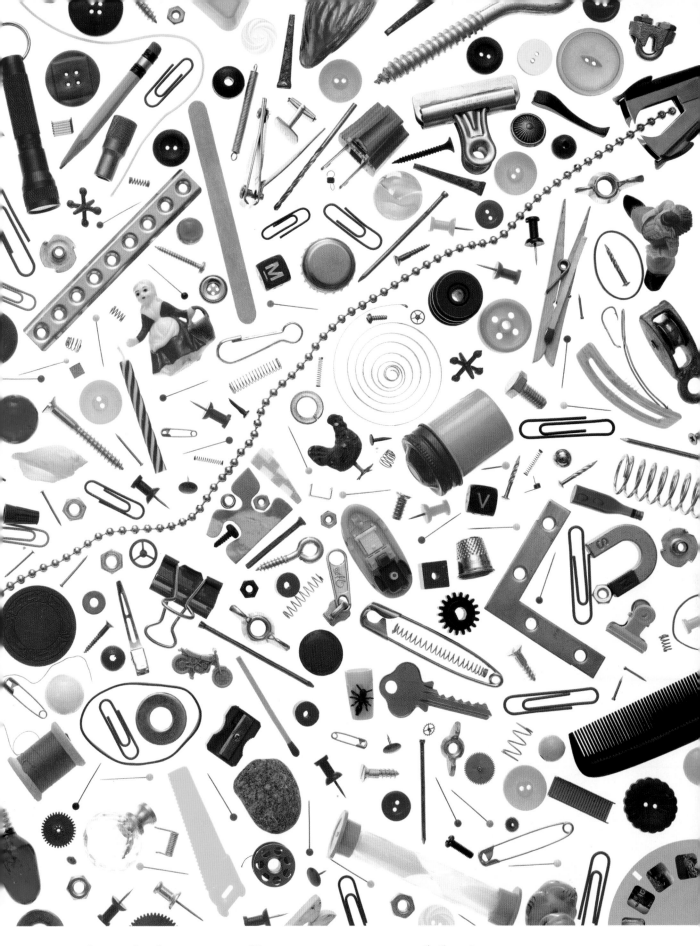

A birthday candle, a pretty gold ring,
A small puzzle piece, and a crown for a king.

I spy a starfish, the feather of a bird,
Thirty-one cents, and a very SANDY word;

A little baby's footprint, a rattle with bells,
A crab, a fork, and seven seashells.

I spy a snake, a three-letter word,
And flying underneath, a great white bird;

Nine gold stars, a blue tube of glitter,
One clay cat, and a six-legged critter.

I spy a stamp, a boy with a plane,
A key on a ring, a song about rain;

Two striped socks, a spaghetti-sauce face,
A girl on a swing, and a snowcapped place.

I spy a wand and ballet slippers,
A bird on a scarf, and fingernail clippers;

A bunny-rabbit mask, a heart-shaped box,
A birthday candle, and a key that locks.

I spy an arrowhead, a little white goose,
A horse's shadow, a snake on the loose;

One egg that's white, another that's blue,
A tiger in the grass, and a small turtle, too.

I spy a lamb, a small silver jack,
A bright yellow pencil, a blue thumbtack;

Two black arrows, a red ladybug,
A little puppy dog, and an Oriental rug.

I spy a clothespin, one silver dime,
A little round face that used to tell time;

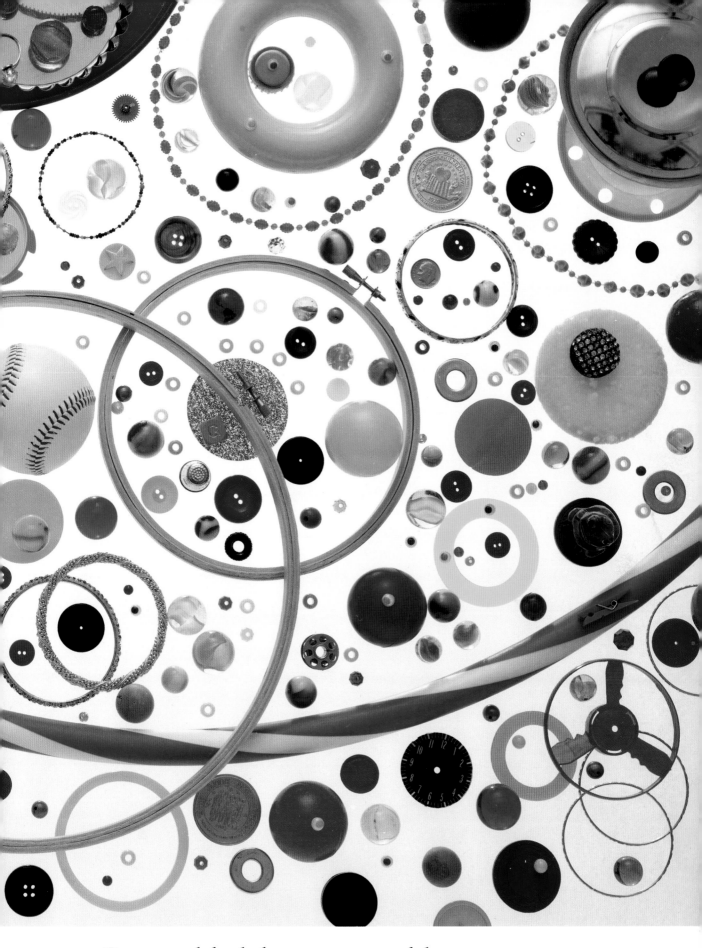

One red ladybug, one gold star;
A new baseball, and a wheel for a car.

I spy a squirt gun, a cowboy hat,
Six airplanes, and a baseball bat;

The point of a pencil, a whistle with a star,
Two yo-yos, and a screw near a car.

I spy an eagle, eleven fish with fins,
A yellow paper clip, and ten bowling pins;

A bright red phone, a pink baby shoe,
A spider that's black, and an eight that's blue.

I spy an anchor, a musical note,
A crayon and a snake and a small billy goat;

A pair of sunglasses, a tiny bird cage —
I also spy something from every other page.

EXTRA CREDIT RIDDLES

"Find Me" Riddle

I'm little and green; I live in a bog;
I'm in every picture; I am a _____.

Find the Pictures That Go with These Riddles:

I spy six matches, an electric plug,
A double-decker cone, and a little black bug.

I spy a squirrel, a small blue pail,
A penny in a boat, and one little nail.

I spy three hearts, a bat and a ball,
One king's crown, and five 5's in all.

I spy a jar, a small striped stone,
An old flowerpot, and antlers of bone.

I spy a butterfly, a little pearl ring,
One king's crown, and a toy with a string.

I spy a fish and a small cutting tool,
A craftstick doll, and thread on a spool.

I spy a swan, two silly clowns,
An Indian chief, and two gold crowns.

I spy a blimp, an American flag,
A silver safety pin, and a small price tag.

I spy a seahorse, a lonely flip-flop,
A little fisherman, and a buried bottle top.

I spy a reindeer, a colorful parrot,
A thimble with a plant, and a little orange carrot.

I spy a fishhook nearby a hen,
An elephant, egg, and a ballpoint pen.

I spy a clown and a pretty white glove,
A small white horse, and a couple in love.

I spy a globe, an upside-down heart,
Three sports trophies, and a little red cart.

Write Your Own Picture Riddles

There are many more hidden objects and many more possibilities for riddles in this book. Write some rhyming picture riddles yourself, and try them out with friends.

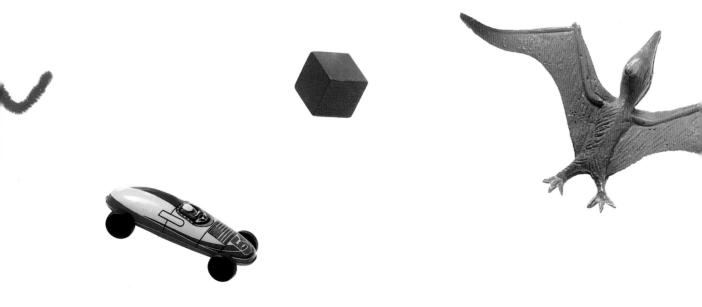

Walter Wick is the award-winning photographer of the I Spy series as well as the author and photographer of the bestselling Can You See What I See? series. His other books include *A Ray of Light: A Book of Science and Wonder* and *A Drop of Water: A Book of Science and Wonder*. He has created photographs for books, magazines, and newspapers. Walter's photographs have been featured in museums around the United States. He lives with his wife, Linda, in Miami Beach, Florida.

More information about Walter Wick is available at walterwick.com and scholastic.com/canyouseewhatisee.

Jean Marzollo was the author of over a hundred books, including the bestselling I Spy series; *Help Me Learn Numbers 0–20*; *Help Me Learn Addition*; *Help Me Learn Subtraction*; and *I Am Water*; as well as books for parents and teachers, such as *The New Kindergarten*. Her sons, Dan and Dave, helped Jean write some of the newer I Spy books. Jean made sure that every riddle in every I Spy book was rich with concrete words that children could understand and that those words were set in an inviting pattern of rhythm and rhyme. For more information, go to scholastic.com/ispy.

Carol Devine Carson, the book designer, has designed covers for books by John Updike, Joan Didion, Alice Munro, and many more. For nineteen years, Marzollo and Carson produced Scholastic's kindergarten magazine, *Let's Find Out*.